Franklin Stays Up

From an episode of the animated TV series *Franklin*, produced by Nelvana Limited, Neurones France s.a.r.l. and Neurones Luxembourg S.A., based on the Franklin books by Paulette Bourgeois and Brenda Clark.

Story written by Sharon Jennings.

Illustrated by Sean Jeffrey, Shelley Southern and Jelena Sisic.

Based on the TV episode *Franklin Stays Up*, written by Brian Lasenby.

 is a trademark of Kids Can Press Ltd.

Franklin is a trademark of Kids Can Press Ltd.
The character Franklin was created by Paulette Bourgeois and Brenda Clark.
Text © 2003 Contextx Inc.
Illustrations © 2003 Brenda Clark Illustrator Inc.

Kids Can Press acknowledges the financial support of the Ontario Arts Council, the Canada Council for the Arts and the Government of Canada, through the BPIDP, for our publishing activity.

Published in Canada by
Kids Can Press Ltd.
29 Birch Avenue
Toronto, ON M4V 1E2

Published in the U.S. by
Kids Can Press Ltd.
2250 Military Road
Tonawanda, NY 14150

www.kidscanpress.com

Edited by Tara Walker
Designed by Stacie Bowes

Printed in Hong Kong, China, by Wing King Tong Company Limited

CM 03 0 9 8 7 6 5 4 3 2 1
CM PA 03 0 9 8 7 6 5 4 3 2 1

National Library of Canada Cataloguing in Publication Data

Jennings, Sharon
      Franklin stays up / Sharon Jennings ; illustrated by Sean Jeffrey, Jelena Sisic, Shelley Southern.

(Kids Can read)
The character Franklin was created by Paulette Bourgeois and Brenda Clark.

ISBN 1-55337-371-5 (bound).   ISBN 1-55337-372-3 (pbk.)

I. Bourgeois, Paulette II. Clark, Brenda III. Jeffrey, Sean IV. Sisic, Jelena
V. Southern, Shelley VI. Title. VII. Series: Kids Can read (Toronto, Ont.)

PS8569.E563F7325 2003   jC813'.54   C2002-902090-5
PZ7

Kids Can Press is a *Corus*™ Entertainment company

Franklin Stays Up

Kids Can Press

Franklin can tie his shoes.

Franklin can count by twos.

And Franklin can stay up

until nine o'clock.

But one night, Franklin wanted

to stay up past nine o'clock.

"I'm not tired,"

Franklin told his mother.

"You may stay up a little bit longer,"

she said.

"I want to stay up a lot longer,"

said Franklin.

"I want to stay up all night long."

"And what will you do all night long?"

asked his mother.

"I will have lots and lots of fun,"

said Franklin.

But by ten o'clock,

Franklin was asleep.

In the morning,

Franklin had a good idea.

He went to find his friends.

"I want to have a stay-up-over

in my tent," he said.

"You mean a sleepover," said Bear.

"No," said Franklin.

"I mean a stay-up-over.

We will stay up all night long."

"I can bring food," said Bear.

"I can bring games," said Rabbit.

"I can bring a radio," said Snail.

"Good," said Franklin.

"We will have fun all night long."

Everyone came to Franklin's house after supper.

Franklin put up the tent.

Bear put out the food.

Rabbit put out the games.

Snail turned on the radio.

"Now we're ready to stay up

all night long," said Franklin.

At nine o'clock, Franklin's parents came

to say good night.

"We're not going to bed,"

said Franklin.

"But *we* are," said his mother.

"We have to get up early

to make you a pancake breakfast."

"Hooray!" said everyone.

"Have fun," said Franklin's father.

"What will we do now?" asked Snail.

"Let's eat," said Bear.

"Let's play tag, then eat," said Franklin.

Everyone ran around and around

the backyard.

"I'm tired," said Bear.

"No! No! No!" said Franklin.

"You can't get tired.

We have to stay up all night long."

"Okay," said Bear.

"Let's eat the popcorn."

By ten o'clock, all the popcorn was gone.

"Let's play chess," said Rabbit.

Everyone started to play.

Soon, Rabbit started to yawn.

"Hurry up and move,"

Rabbit told Snail.

"I'm falling asleep."

"No! No! No!" said Franklin.

"You can't fall asleep.

We have to stay up all night long."

"Okay," said Rabbit.

"Let's eat the cookies."

By twelve o'clock,

all the cookies were gone.

"Let's tell spooky stories," said Snail.

Everyone took turns

telling spooky stories.

"I'm scared," said Snail.

"I want to go home."

"No! No! No!" said Franklin.

"You can't go home.

We have to stay up all night long."

"Okay," said Snail.

"Is there anything left to eat?"

But there was nothing left to eat.

"Let's go inside and find some food," said Franklin.

Everyone tiptoed into the house.

"Look!" said Rabbit.

"The table is set for our pancake breakfast."

"I can hardly wait," said Bear.

"Just a few more hours," said Franklin.

"It's already one o'clock!"

Franklin found bread and jam

in the cupboard.

Then everyone tiptoed outside.

They made sandwiches in the tent.

"I'm all sticky," said Snail.

"Me too," said Bear.

"I know what to do," said Franklin.

"Follow me."

Franklin turned on the hose.

Everyone got wet.

"I'm c-c-cold," said Snail.

He got into his sleeping bag.

"Me t-t-too," said Bear.

He got into his sleeping bag.

Snail yawned and fell asleep.

Bear yawned and fell asleep.

"Oh, no," said Franklin.

"This is not a good stay-up-over."

Franklin and Rabbit went outside

and counted stars.

"One, two — *yawn* — three," said Rabbit.

"Four, five, six," said Franklin.

"This is — *yawn, yawn* — just like

counting sheep," said Rabbit.

"Seven, eight, nine," said Franklin.

Yawn, yawn, yawn, went Rabbit.

Then he fell asleep.

"Oh, no," said Franklin.

Franklin looked at his alarm clock.

It was three o'clock in the morning.

Then Franklin yawned.

"No! No! No!" he said.

"I can't fall asleep.

I have to stay up all night long!"

Franklin ran

around and around

the yard.

He did jumping jacks.

He turned on

the radio.

He held his eyes
wide open.
Just when Franklin
knew he couldn't
stay up one minute longer,
he saw the sun.

"Hooray!" said Franklin.

"I stayed up all night long!"

Then he fell asleep.

At nine o'clock, Franklin's mother
went outside.

"Wake up," she called.

"It's time for breakfast!"

Snail woke up.

Bear woke up.

Rabbit woke up.

Franklin did not wake up.

"Franklin! Franklin! Franklin!"

said Snail and Bear and Rabbit.

"The pancakes are ready."

Franklin yawned and rolled over.

"I don't want any pancakes," he said.

"I want to sleep all day long."